D1735969

Sheep

Sharon Dalgleish

This edition first published in 2005 in the United States of America by Chelsea Clubhouse, a division of Chelsea House Publishers and a subsidiary of Haights Cross Communications.

Chelsea House Publishers
2080 Cabot Boulevard West, Suite 201
Langhorne, PA 19047-1813

The Chelsea House world wide web address is www.chelseahouse.com

First published in 2005 by
MACMILLAN EDUCATION AUSTRALIA PTY LTD
627 Chapel Street, South Yarra, Australia, 3141

Associated companies and representatives throughout the world.

Visit our website at www.macmillan.com.au

Library of Congress Cataloging-in-Publication Data

Dalgleish, Sharon.
Sheep / Sharon Dalgleish.
p. cm. -- (Farm animals)
Includes index.
ISBN 0-7910-8271-7
1. Sheep--Juvenile literature. I. Title.
SF375.2.D35 2004
636.3--dc22

2004016191

Edited by Ruth Jelley
Text and cover design by Christine Deering
Page layout by Domenic Lauricella
Photo research by Legend Images

Printed in China

Acknowledgments
The author and the publisher are grateful to the following for permission to reproduce copyright material:

Cover photograph: sheep and lambs, courtesy of Photolibrary.com.

Australian Picture Library, p. 20 (top); Australian Picture Library/Corbis, pp. 23, 26; Corbis Digital Stock, p. 7; The DW Stock Picture Library, pp. 6, 16, 21 (top), 22; Getty Images/Photodisc, pp. 3, 8 (center and bottom); Image Library, p. 19 (top); Bill Belson/Lochman Transparencies, p. 5; Dennis Sarson/Lochman Transparencies, p. 19 (bottom); Len Stewart/Lochman Transparencies, p. 27; G. R. Roberts © Natural Sciences Image Library, pp. 25 (top and bottom), 28; © Peter E. Smith, Natural Sciences Image Library, pp. 8 (top), 9; Pelusey Photography, pp. 24 (top and bottom); Photodisc, p. 4; Photolibrary.com, pp. 1, 10, 11, 12, 13, 14, 15, 18, 20 (bottom), 21 (bottom); Stockbyte, p. 17; United States Department of Agriculture, p. 30.

While every care has been taken to trace and acknowledge copyright, the publisher tenders their apologies for any accidental infringement where copyright has proved untraceable. Where the attempt has been unsuccessful, the publisher welcomes information that would redress the situation.

Contents

What Is a Sheep?

A sheep is an animal with a thick coat of wool called a **fleece**. This fleece can be white, black, or brown. Sheep make a bleating "baa" sound.

Sheep may all sound the same, but they can tell each other apart.

The adult female sheep is a called a ewe. The adult male is called a ram. The young are called lambs. A group of sheep is called a flock.

Sheep stay together in a flock.

Ewes

Ewes give birth to lambs. The new lamb follows its mother everywhere. If a lamb strays from its mother, the mother bleats until they find each other.

Lambs have their tails shortened when they are between one and three months old.

Rams

Sometimes rams fight. They stamp their feet. Then they step back, lower their heads, and charge. They bang horns and heads together with a loud crash.

Rams have hard skulls and can hurt each other.

Life Cycle

Lambs grow up to have lambs of their own, and the life cycle continues.

Lambs are very thin when they are first born. They drink milk from their mother and grow quickly.

Lambs are fully grown at six months. But they are still called lambs until they are one year old.

Adult rams and ewes **mate** to produce lambs. The ewe gives birth to one, or sometimes two, lambs at a time.

Lambs

Lambs are wet when they are born and are licked clean by their mother.

Licking helps to form a bond between the ewe and her lambs.

Lambs

By the time the lamb is one hour old it can stand, walk, and drink milk from its mother. It butts the ewe's **udder** with its head to make the milk flow.

The lamb wags its tail as it drinks.

When lambs are a few weeks old, they start to nibble grass. They continue to drink milk from their mother. They stay with her until they no longer need her milk.

Lambs stay with their mother until they are about four months old.

Farm Life

Farmers keep sheep in open fields. Sheep spend the day eating and resting. The ewes and lambs are easily frightened so they stay together in a flock.

Ewes and lambs stay together for safety.

There are usually a lot more ewes than rams on a farm. The rams often live in a separate field. They join the rest of the flock only at breeding time.

Farmers keep fewer rams than ewes.

Eating

Sheep eat grass, leaves, twigs, and young plants. They don't have front teeth on the top jaw. This helps them get closer to the ground to **graze**.

Sheep eat short grass because it is easy to nibble.

A sheep's stomach has four sections. Food is stored in the first section. Later, the sheep brings the food back up to chew it again. This is called chewing the **cud**.

Sheep sit down when they are chewing the cud.

Playing

Lambs play games and chase each other. Their favorite play time is early morning or late afternoon when it is cooler. But they always stay close to their mother.

Lambs play together with their mothers nearby.

Sleeping

Sheep sleep for only three to four hours a day. They don't all go to sleep at the same time. There are always some sheep still awake to warn the flock of danger.

Sheep don't sleep very much, but they do rest a lot.

Sheep Farming

Some farmers keep sheep for their meat. Meat from a young sheep is called lamb. Meat from an older sheep is called mutton. Ewes can also be milked.

Roquefort cheese is made using milk from ewes.

Other farms keep sheep for their wool. Wool can be made into cloth and yarn, which are used to make clothes. Woolen clothes keep you cool in summer and warm in winter.

Wool can be dyed different colors.

Firefighters wear woolen uniforms because wool doesn't burn easily.

Sheep Breeds

Farmers keep different **breeds** of sheep for different purposes.

Southdown sheep are mainly kept for meat.

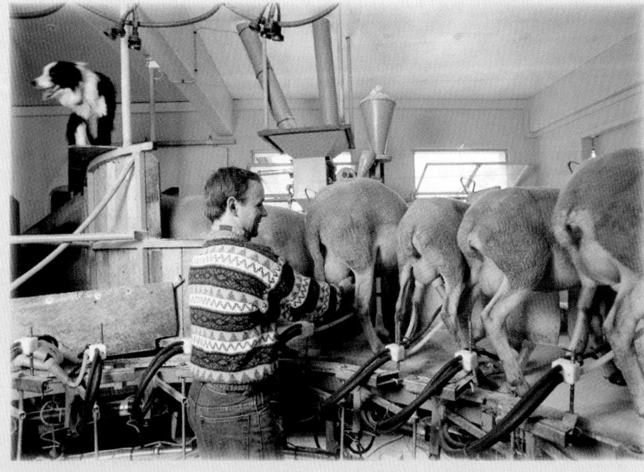

East Friesian dairy sheep are German sheep bred for milk.

Some breeds have fine wool, some have coarse wool, and some are kept for meat or milk.

Scottish Blackface sheep have coarse wool that is used to make carpets.

Australian Merino sheep are famous for their fine, thick wool. Their wool is used to make fine woolen fabric, and is very valuable.

Looking After Sheep

Farmers make sure their fields have plenty of grass for the sheep to eat. If there is no grass, the farmer may feed the sheep grains, such as oats.

During a drought, the farmer might give the sheep oats, wheat, or barley.

Sheep also need plenty of water to drink. Sometimes the water is pumped to the water troughs from a **dam**.

Sheep need drinking water to stay healthy.

Rounding Up

Sheep need to be rounded up and checked closely a few times a year.

Stage 1

First, the farmer uses a motorbike to move around the field and find all the sheep.

Stage 2

Next, herding dogs help steer the sheep to the fence line.

Most farmers use motorbikes and dogs to round up the sheep and move them all together to a sheep yard.

Stage 3

Then, the farmer and dog walk the sheep along the fence line toward the gate.

Stage 4

Finally, the sheep are safely in the yard.

Dipping

Most farmers "dip" their sheep twice a year. The sheep are made to swim in a special mixture to kill pests such as ticks. Even the sheep's head must be dipped under.

The farmer dips the sheep's head into the special mixture.

Shearing

Shearing is when sheep have their wool cut off. The wool is cut off keeping the fleece in one piece. It takes about a year for a sheep's fleece to grow back fully.

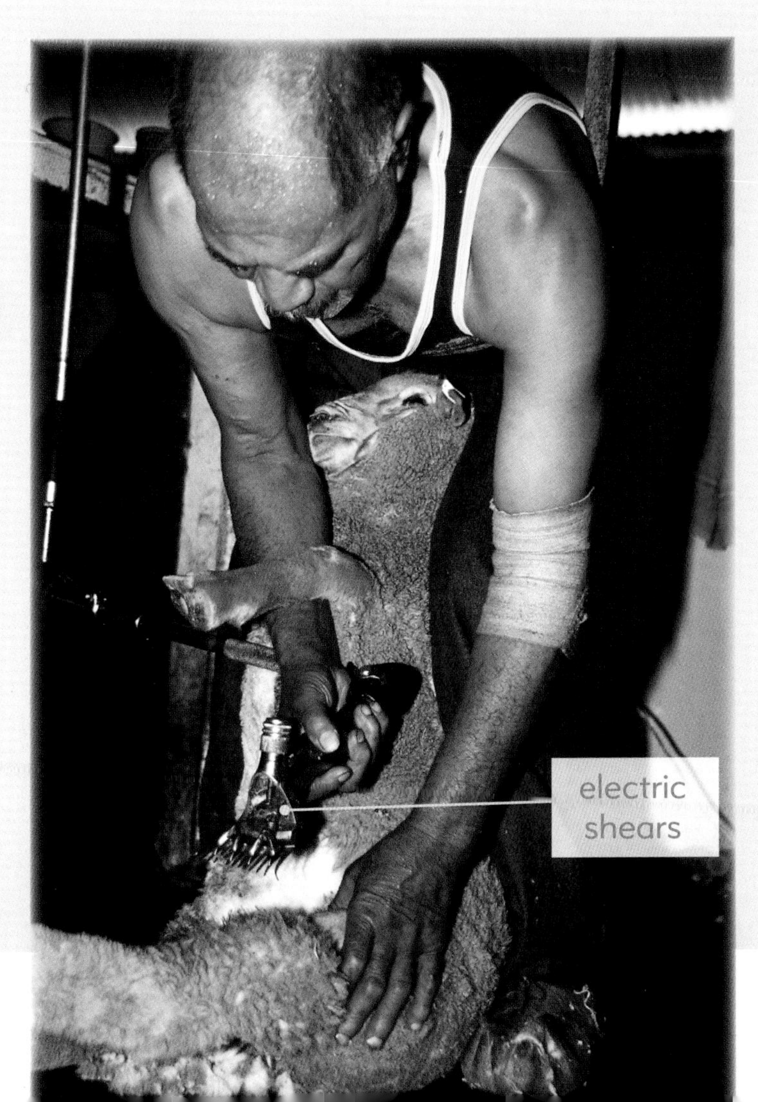

The wool is cut off using special electric shears.

Sorting Sheep

Farmers sometimes need to sort their sheep into two groups. Farmers move the flock down a race, which has two gates at the end to separate the groups.

The gates can move either way to sort the sheep.

How to Tell the Age of a Sheep

What to do

1. Look at the sheep's front teeth. These are all **incisors**.
2. Count the large adult teeth, not the baby teeth.
3. Check against this table to see how old the sheep is.

Adult Incisors	Age
2 incisors	1 year old
4 incisors	2 years old
6 incisors	3 years old
8 incisors	4 years old
8 incisors, close together	5 years old
8 incisors, spread apart	6 years old
some incisors broken	7 to 8 years old
all incisors missing	10 to 12 years old

Farm Facts

- If a sheep tumbles onto its back it cannot get up again on its own.
- A fleece can weigh between 4 and 20 pounds, depending on the breed of the sheep.
- A good shearer can shear a sheep in five minutes. That makes up to 125 sheep in a day. The world record for shearing is 805 sheep in 9 hours. That's 89 sheep per hour.
- A ewe can give up to 46 gallons of milk in 12 weeks.

Glossary

breed	a group of animals that have the same set of features
cud	small lump of half-chewed grass inside a sheep's stomach
dam	a pond that stores water on a farm
fleece	a coat of wool that covers a sheep's body
graze	to feed on growing grass
incisor	a tooth in the front of the mouth, used for cutting
mate	when a male and female join to create their young
udder	a ewe's milk bag

Index